This way please!

Dear Miss

By Amy Husband

For James

Published in 2014
by Albury Children's Books
Albury Court, Albury
OX9 2LP, United Kingdom
Illustrations © Amy Husband
Text © Rachel Elliot

The rights of Amy Husband and Rachel Elliot to be identified as the illustrator
and author of this work have been asserted
by them in accordance with the Copyright,
Designs and Patents Act, 1988

A CIP catalogue record for this book
is available from the British Library
10 9 8 7 6 5 4 3 2 1
Printed in China

D1411952

Albury Children's

Sunnybank Primary School

Friday 15th August

Dear Michael,

We are looking forward to welcoming you back to school for the start of the new term. I hope you have had a really fun break and are ready to dive into lots of learning!

This year your class will be working especially hard in math, history, geography and English. I am sure that if you study carefully, you will find those spelling tests can be a fun challenge!

Your new teacher is called Miss Brooks. She has all sorts of exciting plans for the new term. We look forward to seeing you on Monday.

Yours sincerely,

N.T Grindstone

Mr N.T. Grindstone
Headmaster

the secret service man

Dear Miss,
I might be a bit late for the first day of school. The weirdest thing happened today. The head of the **secret service** turned up! They need me for a special **secret** mission to find a missing explorer. I did mention the Math test, but he just said that the future of the country depends on me. I couldn't say no. **Sorry Miss.**

(Fingers crossed I'll be back in time for the test!)

From Michael

My dog Bruno

P.S. Bruno's coming with me — he makes a great bloodhound.

P.P.S. The stuff I've told you is **Top Secret**, so please eat this letter.

TOP SECRET

Royal Mail

Missing Explorer

Dear Miss,

The explorer was stuck on top of <u>Mount Everest!</u> We rescued him and Bruno was brilliant! I've never seen a dog go that fast before.

The explorer told me about an ancient treasure map hidden in **Egypt**. He has a bad cold, so he wants me to search for the map.

(I did tell him I had to get back for the math test, but this is <u>really important.</u>)

To the summit 2 miles

I will probably only be a few hours late for the first day of school.

From **Michael**

P.S. Please don't let Nicholas sit in my place.

Mountain Mail

Honest, Miss, I didn't know it was going to the Amazon River! The map says the treasure is hidden there so I might as well find it.

From Michael

P.S. I'll really miss the homework.

TELEGRAM

MISS.

AMAZON VERY **HOT** AND DANGEROUS.

NO SIGN OF TREASURE.

SORRY ABOUT RIPPED PAPER.   ATTACKED BY CROC.

LIVING OFF BEETLES AND SPIDERS.

REALLY MISS PEANUT BUTTER SANDWICHES.

WILL BE EVEN LATER NOW.

HIPPO ATE COMPASS.

MICHAEL.

P.S. OH NO! SNAKES CAN SWIM!

It was hidden behind a waterfall, not by a river! Bruno had been holding the map the wrong way. (Never trust a dog with a map.)

We'll start for home as soon as we can find some transport. The bad news is, I'll be really late for the start of school, sorry.

From **Michael**

P.S. This is all still TOP SECRET so don't tell anyone.

Dear Miss,

We found a boat home but Pirates **attacked** us! The Pirate King tied us up, stole the treasure and made us **walk the plank!** Thank goodness Bruno and I are such good swimmers. I'm going to get the treasure back. This could make me really **really late!** I'm really sorry, Miss, but I can't let the Pirate King get away with this.

From Michael

P.S. Please don't let Nicholas use my felt tips.

P.P.S. I don't mind if he takes my turn at tidying the storage cupboard.

Dear Miss,
We found out where the
pirates are going and we've
hired an airplane to try to
cut them off. Wish us luck!
We'll be a bit longer than I thought,
but don't worry, Miss, ~~bird~~ I can't
wait to catch up on all the work.

From **Michael**

P.S. Bruno makes a brilliant co-pilot,
except when he tries to chase birds.· · ·

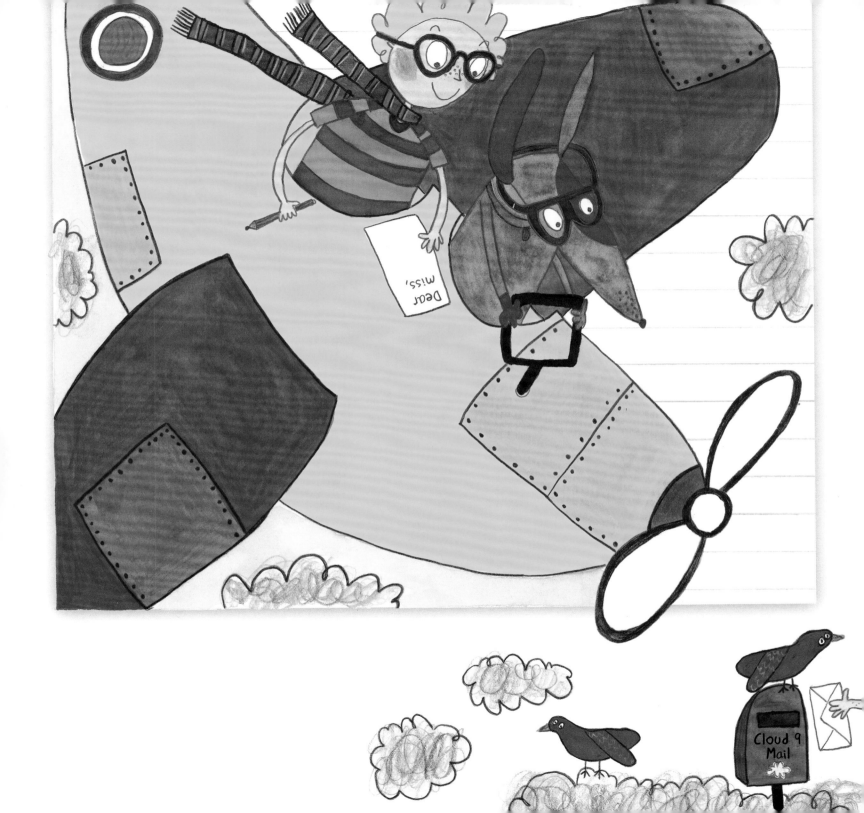

From Michael

P.S. It's probably best not to mention this to Mom if you see her in the supermarket again.

Orient Express
Platform 3
←————————≪

Express
Mail

Dear Miss,

I've got some good news and some bad news. We caught the Pirate King trying to steal a rocket! Bruno and I stopped him though. Now for the bad news. I'm not going to be coming back ever. I'm really disappointed (especially about the science test.)

NASA want me to go on a space mission. I'll be on the moon for a gazilion years. I told them about the math tests, but they said that the future of the planet has to come first. Bruno's coming too, so I won't be lonely.